I DON'T WANT TO TURN 3

GRAMPS JEFFREY

AuthorHouse™
1663 Liberty Drive
Bloomington, IN 47403
www.authorhouse.com
Phone: 833–262–8899

This book is printed on acid–free paper.

ISBN: 978–1–6655–2693–7 (sc)
ISBN: 978–1–6655–2694–4 (hc)
ISBN: 978–1–6655–2692–0 (e)

Library of Congress Control Number: 2021910573

Print information available on the last page.

Published by AuthorHouse 05/24/2021

authorHOUSE®

I Don't Want to Turn 3

By: Gramps Jeffrey

My name is Jordan, and I am going to turn 3 tomorrow. Once I turn 3, my parents are going to expect so much more from me... and I am very scared of that.

You see, when I am 2, I can do just about anything I want and get away with it. For instance, my cousin Jackson has these dinosaurs, the Tyrannosaurus Rex, the Spinosaurus and the Stegosaurus. Because I wanted them, I just pulled them out of his hands and ran off with them. Jackson's Mommy told him that because I was just 2, let me keep them. Jackson cried, but the dinosaurs are now mine.

Last night I was taking a bath with my other cousin Levi and we had all of his sea creatures like whales, squids, crabs and turtles swimming in the tub with us. While Levi was getting his hair washed, I grabbed all of the sea creatures and sat on them so no one could see them.

When Levi asked where his sea creatures were, I told him they swam down the drain. Levi jumped out of the tub and ran all over the house looking for his sea creatures. While he was running and screaming, I took the sea creatures and hid them underneath my pajamas. To this day, Levi is still looking for his sea creatures, which are now mine in a big pile with my dinosaurs.

This morning, I went to the park with my little 1 year old brother Baker. For Baker's first birthday, Daddy had bought him lots of trucks like a dump truck, a fire truck and a garbage truck. So like a good big brother, I taught Baker how to roll the trucks back and forth on the sidewalk at the park. He was so happy that I was playing with him, that he had a smile that went from ear to ear.

After we got home, he went for his nap and I snatched up all of his new trucks. Baker is so little; I don't think he will ever remember I took all of his stuff. And now— his trucks are in the same pile as my new dinosaurs and sea creatures!

I also have a little 2-year-old girl cousin named Grace. Grace loves baby dolls. She spends almost every waking hour feeding her dolls, dressing her dolls and combing her dolls hair. I personally don't like dolls, but because we are cousins and sometimes are forced to be together since we are only 1 year apart, I have to sit next to Grace and tell her I like her baby dolls (which I really don't so I guess this is the first lie I tell in my life).

But being who I truly am, when Grace is not looking, I begin to take her dolls and hide them behind the chair. By the end of the morning, I have 5 dolls, and yes you guessed it, they are now on my pile of trucks and dinosaurs and sea creatures.

I do have a wise old 8—year—old cousin, Olivia. She wants to become a professional dancer, so is always swooshing and bending and dancing around me. Last week Olivia and I went to the zoo with Grandma. I loved the lions, hippopotamus, and elephant; and Olivia loved the flamingos, swans, and giraffes. Grandma bought me a bag of animals. I did not share them with anyone. When we got home and Olivia was not looking, I took her dancing shoes; and they are now on the top of the pile of dolls and trucks and dinosaurs and sea creatures and zoo animals.

Tomorrow is now today, and I am officially celebrating being 3 years old. All of my family is at our house. I just blew out the 3 candles on the cake and started to open the birthday presents my cousins brought me. Levi's family gave me a bunch of shark toys to include the Hammerhead Shark, the Great White Shark, and the Tiger Shark. Jackson's family got me a toy tow truck and a concrete mixer.

Then all of a sudden Olivia screams "what are my dancing shoes doing in Jordan's room?" The entire family runs to my private bedroom and Jackson yells "my dinosaurs" and Levi shrieks "my sea creatures" and Baker bawls "truck" and Grace cries "my dolls". And Mommy looks at me like today will be my last day alive.

As my cousins' surge at me ready to pounce, Daddy steps between them and me and says "I see you are all quite mad at your cousin Jordan. Let's sit down in a circle and work this out". Whoa, that was close...but everyone listened to Daddy and sat down. "I want everyone to take a deep breath and begin to calm down" said Dad. He looked at me and said, "it is time to put on your problem−solving hat". He looked at all of us kids and said, "it is time to decide for yourself what is right and what is wrong". Jackson says, "I feel angry when my dinosaurs are grabbed from my hands without asking me− Please don't do that". Levi says, "when my sea creatures are hidden from me, I get very frustrated and upset and don't know what to do".

"Who knows what the word sharing means", asks Dad. Wise old cousin Olivia says, "when you play together with your toys, everyone gets to have fun. Our toys are for everyone. It's ours, it is not just Jackson's or Levi's or Jordan's. I learned when I was 5 that when you play with your friends and share, everyone has a good time".

Dad looks at me and asks if I had anything I wanted to share with the group. I said no because I felt so guilty that I got caught. So, Dad just stared at me for what seemed like hours and said, "today as you turn 3, you must learn what it means to be kind, and as important fair'.

Olivia than exclaimed, "I know what we should do. Let's give the entire pile of toys and the toys Jordan just got for his birthday to the homeless shelter kids downtown. My school is having a toy drive to help the less fortunate".

The room fell silent. No one really wanted to give up their toys. Dad said to me "the biggest lesson you can learn on your birthday is caring about others and showing compassion for those not as fortunate as you and your cousins". Now I am only 3 years old, so I did not quite understand what Daddy meant, but in his eyes and with his smile I could see he was telling me that this is the right thing to do.

I looked at Jackson, then Levi, then Baker, then Grace and finally Olivia. "OK" is what I said, and the rest of the cousins then said "OK". Together we started putting our dinosaurs, our sea creatures, our trucks, our zoo animals, and our dolls into a box Daddy pulled out of the closet. I also took my birthday gifts and put them into the box.

I was really sad that all of that effort of hiding the toys together in my room did not work. But at the same time, to see my parents so pleased with what we are doing to help others, made me really glad. I guess that is the difference between being 2 and being 3— one day, you only think about yourself and the next you actually think of other people...

CPSIA information can be obtained
at www.ICGtesting.com
Printed in the USA
LVHW070602150621
690251LV00020B/1330